Losing Her

A King Family Christmas Novella

Book Five

A King Family Series

AUTHOR. DREAMER. WANDERER

The King Family has been through turmoil and suffered many losses these past couple of years. Yet, they've grown. In numbers. In wealth. In power.

They've grown stronger and closer.

With the family still recovering from the fallout between Derrick and Stella, find out if the holidays can bring them back together. After all, it's the most wonderful time of the year, isn't it?

With a strong alliance keeping their borders and their business busy, there's bound to be more than one guest appearance for the holidays. See how the Kings welcome their friends and bless their foes in the first King Family Christmas novella.

TABLE OF CONTENTS

Chapter
ONE

"*Vodka chistaya,*" Peter Ivanov tells the bartender as he uninvitingly takes the seat next to his own.

The man's voice grated on his nerves worse than the scraping of the bar stool from beside him scraping against the floor. Fucking great. Why the fuck would Peter think it'd be okay to sit down? They barely tolerated each other.

He tosses back the last of the whiskey neat in his tumbler and signals for the bartender to bring him another as she pours the vodka shot for Peter. Her red-lipped smile and wink say she'd pour a whole bottle of whiskey down his throat if she could. An inebriated King might be easier to tame.

Fat fucking chance.

One slip with that was enough. One slip and he's here in a bar with Peter Ivanov.

The bartender slides their drinks in front of them with one hell of a seductive smile.

He frowns at the drink in front of him as if it's turned into a coiled snake ready to strike. He can feel Ivanov's eyes burning a hole into his side so he turns to face the Russian prick.

Peter doesn't say anything. The asshole simply stares at him in confusion then reaches inside his pocket to tip the bartender. Peter waves her away with the flick of his fingers.

She looked a bit shocked that her company wasn't requested especially since the bar is half dead. But she saunters off, swaying her hips way too hard for it to be normal.

"What do you want?" he growls out to Peter when they are alone.

"*Chto zabralos' tebe v zadnitsu?*" Peter snarks at him. *What got up your ass?*

"I'm not Carter," he grunts back because thanks to his cousin, Peter Ivanov has been getting too comfortable lately.

"*Dah*, thaz right." Peter chuckles. "Waz asking what's crawled up your ass," he says with a lax accent before tossing back the vodka.

"Fucking Christmas," he mumbles before he could stop himself. He must have had one too many neats already.

"Don't be a coward, King," Peter taunts him.

He glares at Peter with his hands in fists, ready to go at it. Truth be told, he's been ready to go at it with Peter for a very long time now but it's unclear why he hasn't yet. Okay. It's pretty clear. Even with the fucking fact that this motherfucker wants Stella all to himself,

Peter Ivanov has saved her one too many times. Ivanov has been man enough to respect Stella's decision as well.

"*Moya malenk'kaya zvezda?*" Peter continues unfazed by the heat brewing between them.

THAT...he understood. "She's MY wife! Not YOUR little star. She's not YOUR anything!" he warns the man.

"*Nyet!* She is MY queen! One who I would walk fires for if she had so chosen me! You put her in cages of gold but cannot keep her happy. And you do NOTHING to change that," Peter snarls at him.

"What the fuck do you know about it?" he says through gritted teeth. He can feel the vein in his neck pulsing in anger. His blood is boiling like hot lava ready to erupt.

What the fuck does this Bratva Prince know anything about what's happened between Stella and him to speak out of place? It wouldn't matter that Carter is about to marry Ivanov's sister, his cousin still wouldn't be blabbing about the family business. The Ivanovs are not family. They're barely considered business associates.

He gets up out of his seat this time, his hands balled in fists.

Ivanov's two men flank their boss immediately. They should. They're boss's head my just fucking roll off of his shoulders right now.

He can feel Sully and Tommy step up behind him as well. His men are just as ready.

Peter Ivanov doesn't get out of his seat though. He sits there with a bored look on his sharp face as he traces the tip of his tongue across his upper teeth then lets out a loud whistle. Peter snaps his fingers at his two men and without hesitation, the two lackeys begin clearing people out of the bar.

There isn't a peep of protest as the patrons quickly clear the establishment as if their life depended on it.

"Sweetheart," Peter calls out to the bartender. "Bring us the bottle and take a break, *dah*?"

She quickly follows instructions too, disappearing through one of the exit doors without so much as a glance after she settles the bottle of vodka in front of Peter.

"Sit down. Sit down," Peter says with his eyes rolling. "So sensitive," the asshole mumbles loudly as he waves his men back.

The two goons take a seat towards the back of the bar.

He hears the sound of holsters being unbuckled behind him anyway. His men won't take any chances.

"So tense," Peter jokes with a sneer at Sully and Tommy. Peter holds his tatted hand out to the vacated seat in a gesture for him to sit down. "Do you think Stella would let me live if I harm you?" Peter asks with a scoff.

"You're scared of my wife but not me?" he grumbles then plops down in the seat.

"*Dah,*" Peter answers as he pours the shots. "You break bones. Shoot people here. Shoot people there. *Iz* nothing. Stella? She break hearts and kill souls," Peter says with a shrug and a roll of his Russian accent. "I'd like to keep both things."

The words actually get him to crack a fucking laugh.

"What?" Peter asks. "It's fucking true, *nyet*?"

"I can't disagree," he replies and takes the shot Peter offers to him.

The last thing he thought he'd be doing tonight was to be sitting in a bar and having a heart to heart with Peter Ivanov, the same guy who's been lusting for his wife for almost two years now. Life's a fucking stand-up comedy and sometimes, it feels like he's the brunt of the joke.

"What are you doing here?" he asks Peter.

"I drop Emi and the boys off to visit with Stella and the baby." Peter pauses and eyes him. "At Ben Gaston's penthouse," he finishes after a moment. "Why is she there at not at the safety of your home?" he asks, reverting to his perfect English.

"Complicated," he replies with a single word.

"Complicated?" Peter parrots with an arched brow. "It's the holidays and your wife and son aren't with you. You're sitting in a bar alone and all you can say is *iz complicated*."

So Peter doesn't know what happened which is a good thing of course, but what else is he supposed to say to a mere business associate? It's not like he's going to spill his guts about being drugged and nearly raped...by a woman. A woman that his wife murdered in cold blood yet it still didn't fix the bridge between them.

"I forget you don't like small talk," Peter cuts in.

He shrugs and then pours both of them another shot.

Peter takes his glass and tosses it back, placing the glass on the countertop without so much as a clink.

"You're still married to her, right?" Peter asks.

"That's not going to change so you can stop dreaming," he growls.

Peter chortles at his retort and then sighs loudly afterward as if he's exhausted. "I gave Stella a chose once and lost her," the man says.

"You were never an option," he replies.

"She would have no option if I had taken her," Peter simply tells him. "That's your problem right now."

"Come again?" he asks.

"You give her too many choices, too much time and space for her to stay independent," Peter tells him.

"I love her the way she is. Contrary to what you fucking believe, she isn't in a cage." If anything, she has him in one.

"I'm not saying you need to control every single one of her moves and take away her independence. She would be miserable."

"Then what are you saying?" he asks Peter now. It's fucking ridiculous that he's even asking this man for marital advice.

"There can't be two alphas in the relationship, King. That's what I'm saying," Peter replies while taking a fistful of pretzels from the basket nearby. "I don't know what happened to cause this rift between the two of you but time isn't going to help shit in this case. Take control back."

He let the words sink in for a moment but god al-fucking-mighty do they make sense when they do sink in.

Peter is right.

He'd let Stella run his life for too fucking long.

He did NOTHING wrong with Isabella Romano. Stella did nothing wrong for her to continue to harbor this guilt. And Adam still got his fucking happily ever after with Ariana. It's time to reign her in.

"*Pozhaluysta,*" Peter says while chomping down on the pretzels. *You're welcome.*

Chapter
TWO

Mornings used to be his favorite time of day. He's fucking miserable waking up alone for the past few months though. His bed is empty and the hallways in the wing of his estate are eerily quiet. There are no sounds of his son's crying or laughing. There was a time in his life where he'd reveled in the peace. Now, he finds it hollow and nearly unbearable. It fills like the still air is trying to choke the life out of him.

He begrudgingly takes the stairs of the grand staircase down to the kitchen but laughter stops him on the way. He'd know that sound anywhere and his mood is immediately perked by it, lured to it as a fish caught on a line would be.

He walks into the living room to find Ariana and Adam on the floor, playing with Jazzy and Rian, his baby boy.

"Dada!" Rian immediately exclaims, throwing his fists in the air.

Rian crawls a few feet before stopping to get himself up on his feet and toddles over to him. He meets his son halfway even though he should let Rian get the practice he needs to get better with walking.

"My boy," he gushes as he picks the toddler up.

He places a kiss on his son's head, taking a good whiff of baby magic. He can't help but agree with Stella on the numerous amount of times she'd claimed that Rian's baby smell can cure all illnesses.

"Where's mama?" he asks his son. If Rian is here this early, that means Stella had to be here too.

"She picked Rory up so they could meet down at the pop-up restaurant," Adam answers for Rian.

"Mama go Coco Ro," Rian pouts.

"That's right," he tells his son even though he didn't know she was meeting with Rory. "Mama went with *Uncle* Ro," he tries to correct his son although it's fucking adorable as all hell how Rian speaks of his uncles.

Adam has now become *Dadam* since they are twins and baby boy sometimes gets them confused granted not as often as Jazzy did when she was Rian's age. Uncle Chase is Coco Chay and Uncle Rory, the hardest name for the toddler, has turned into Coco Ro.

"How's that coming along?" he asks Adam when he should be asking his wife but things are so tense and tumultuous between him and Stella that everyday conversation is nearly impossible since she won't even look at him when he does try to speak to her.

Every day the distance between them grows into canyons. It's not just feet being added, it's miles and miles. His only reprieve is knowing that every time their eyes do connect, he can still see the longing in her captivating eyes. It's the hope that he's been hanging on to.

But maybe Peter Ivanov is right. Something has to change. He's given her too much time and space. He's given her too much taste of independence, not that she wasn't independent and free to do as she wished before but she's getting too accustomed to being without him. The longer they stay apart, the harder things are to being fixed.

"The building itself is completely done and ready. We're just waiting on some last-minute centerpieces," Ariana answers him with a warm smile.

"Your artwork?" he asks her.

She nods at him with a grin a mile wide. "Mine and Chase's," she answers proudly.

He gives her a slight smile. It's the best he can do and it makes him feel like the donkey's ass that Chase liked to call him. On one hand, he's immensely happy for Adam for finding Ariana. On the other hand, he barely took the time to get to know his new sister-in-law since she's come into the Kings' household. He must come off as nothing more than abrasive to her but timing was a bitch in this case.

"I'm sure it will look great," he tells her encouragingly.

"Of course," Adam chimes in and then tickles his wife.

Rian, of course, wants in on all that tickling action and squirms out of his arms. The baby hurriedly waddles over to his uncle and new aunt to join in on the fun. Jazzy joins in as well and the four look like the complete happy white-picket-fence family.

Meanwhile, his marriage is shifting slowly but surely as the plate tectonics moving beneath his feet.

He moves over to the couch and plops into it.

"You should take Rian to the restaurant for lunch," Ariana suggests with a gleaming smile.

He looks at her curiously. "But it's not open yet," he says.

"That's true but you are part owner," Ariana tells him. "Stella and Rory are auditioning the final three head chefs today. You can be the tie-breaker if they need."

"That's not a bad idea," Adam adds in.

"No," he replies. "It's not a bad idea at all!"

Since his luck with amnesia, bits and pieces are still coming but the doctors aren't optimistic it will ever return to one hundred percent at this point. It's been too long a time and the experts think that this is as good as it's going to get. He'd come to terms with it because he'd thought he had time to create new memories with Stella. He'd even looked forward to it.

The one thing he knew from the moment he woke up with his memory loss was that the sound of her laughter will always be his favorite song. He managed to follow the sound of her voice back from the brink of death. He'd managed to fall in love with her for the second time in one lifetime by following that alluring voice of hers like he held the keys to a hidden treasure.

"Mama," Rian fusses when the baby hears his mother laughing.

"That's right, Rian. We're here to see Mama," he tells the baby in his arms.

Though he'd seen the original plans for the restaurant, this is the first time he'd set foot inside of it and the near-complete phase. Even though it's a seasonal and small pop-up location, it's no surprise that an extreme amount of thought and effort has been put into it. The place looks fucking amazing with its gold and crimson hues. It's perfect for both the time of year and the various other Kings' theme.

He'd parked right out front this time. He'd told Sully and Tommy that they didn't need to come inside with him and the little King since Brooks is probably inside anyway.

Now that he's walking through the place he can hear Rory's music softly playing from somewhere. Various employees are bustling about with tables and tableware. He isn't sure what they should or shouldn't be doing so he pays them no mind.

Imagine the fucking skid mark on the polished floor left by his shoes when he comes to a dead stop at the door of the kitchen. It causes his son to look up at him in surprise.

Jealousy wasn't something he possessed until Stella.

"Sorry, son," he whispers and pats his son's back softly.

His eyes revert to the sound of her laughter and he watches the fucking prick in the white uniform spoon-feeding his wife. Then he shoves his way through the door.

"STELLA!" he hollers out too loudly. It startles Rian and the baby bursts into hysterics. "Oh, no, no, Ri. Daddy's sorry, okay?" he comforts his son apologetically. "I'm sorry, big boy."

Meanwhile, Stella seems frozen in place and is staring at him as if he were a fucking stranger.

Fuck that! He quickly aims his anger at the fucker with the spoon.

The guy immediately sizes him up and down like a fucking dunce. "The restaurant isn't opened yet," Mr. Spoon spats at him. "Someone! Anyone! Get him out of here!"

At the asshole's holler, Rian cries even louder.

"No!" Stella finally manages to find her voice. "Brad, this is just a misunderstanding."

She rounds the counter and heads over to him, plucking their crying son from his arm. Which is fine. It only allows him to reach for his Glock behind his back.

"Shhh..." she tries to calm Rian and then glowers up at him. "Derrick," she says calmly. Barely. "This is Brad. He's our new head chef."

As if that means shit to him. That's no fucking excuse to be spoon-feeding someone's wife.

"Brad," she says, turning and speaking to the chef. "This is Derrick King."

Ouch. She doesn't even mention the *husband* part.

"King?" Brad chirps, finally putting the spoon down.

"Yeah," he grunts. "Her husband," he informs. "Brought our son for some lunch with his mother. But I guess I was late for that," he says, reining his frustrations in.

Brad opens his mouth and then shuts it. Looking down at the spoon in his hand, Brad probably just figured out why he now has to fucking die.

He eyes the man silently.

"Derrick!" Stella scolds him.

Oh, no. He isn't too happy with her right now either.

She eyes him, not the least bit intimated. He'd normally be proud. But not today. No fucking way is she getting a pass today.

"Brad, why don't you whip us up your best," Stella says to the asshole. She takes the baby and pushes past him through the doorway and into the dining area.

"What the fuck was that about?" he growls from behind her yet he follows her to whichever seat she's leading him to.

"I don't know what you're talking about," she replies without looking at him.

An employee brings a child seat to their table and scurries away quickly. Probably because the tension in the air is the size of an elephant's dick.

"Is this why you've been giving me the cold shoulder harder and harder by the day," he immediately asks Stella. "Because you now have some hotshot, young chef at your service?"

"Derrick!" she whispers loudly. "Stop your hissing in front of Rian."

One look at his son's quivering bottom lip and he's immediately a pile of shit. Donkey shit. Fuck! He feels like he's just fucking everything up by the day lately. Where the fuck does he go from here?

He sits down in his seat and pulls Rian's baby chair closer to him. He brushes his hand over his son's dark hair. It's getting longer but it's feather-soft with large curls. The gesture is enough to put a smile back on Rian's sweet little face.

"There," he says to Rian. "All better."

Ten minutes past an eternity. That's how long it felt like he'd been sitting with Stella...in silence. He should bring up the elephant in the room but what the fuck is that actual elephant? He doesn't even know where to start.

Thank God food starts to arrive. Quickly, each plate is set in front of them. More than enough for it to be lunch but it all seems to appease Rian who's already gleaming at each dish and reaching for food to stuff into his tiny mouth. Stella, of course, hands Rian a glazed carrot first.

Rian takes it and chomps down on it vigorously. He's never met a kid, not that he's met many, but he's never met a kid that liked whole carrots as much as his son does.

"Hey, Ri Ri!" Rory calls from behind them.

His brother grabs a chair and pulls it up to join them...and there goes his planned lunch with his wife and son and the chance for them to start fixing things. One minute turns into another while Stella and Rory continue chatting about the opening.

Stella had gone back to not speaking to him using Rory as an excuse. But he'd caught her eyeing him a few times. It's a fraction encouraging but still frustrating as fuck not knowing what to say or when to interject. So he'd kept busy texting Mason about Brad's upcoming car troubles.

Chapter
THREE

"Stell?" Ben calls out to her.

"Hmm?" she absentmindedly answers while browsing through the restaurant's menu.

After Cael's visit in the penthouse, her friend had helped put Rian down for a nap and then Ben called and asked if she'd like to meet him downstairs for lunch since he was at the hotel anyway. Cael decided to come too. So now, here they are...just the three of them as usual.

"I love having you here and don't take this the wrong way," Ben starts.

She drops the menu and looks at her two friends.

Ben is fidgeting nervously with his menu now and Cael is sipping on his beer and avoiding eye contact which is highly suspicious for her most outspoken friend.

"But..." she urges Ben even though she knew what was coming.

"It's not good for *ye*, lass," Cael cuts in as if the two were consorting behind her back. That doesn't happen unless it's business-related. "We're under two weeks 'til Christmas. *Ye* should be home with *ye* husband, lass. Just like I'm going home *ta* me family."

"I don't mind having you here at all," Ben quickly interjects. "Don't get that twisted. But I agree with McCullen. I'm not particularly fond of your King but Stell...you're newlyweds. You've been living apart longer than you have been living together as husband and wife."

"I-I..." *don't know what to say* is what she was trying to say. But she truly didn't know how to express herself. Everything is a jumbled mess of hurt, confusion, and...guilt.

"Are you throwing in the towel?" Cael asks her point-blank.

"NO! No!" she replies.

"Then what's the *shite* that's keeping *ye* apart? I'm not asking *ye* about Kings' business right now, lass. But I don't see why things *canna* be fixed, here." Cael looks at her sternly.

She knows both of her friends are truly concerned about her. But how can she tell them the full story without divulging what happened? How can she repeat what she saw in that fucking video? How can she describe the pain that she felt while watching her husband nearly be raped; watching her brother-in-law *actually* be raped by that same woman?

How can she explain that it was all her fault?

"Are you reconsidering your choices?" Ben asks her, bringing her thoughts back to the present conversation. Ben watches her, waiting for her answer. "I know your life has seen a shit ton of chaos the past couple of years, Stella. Are you beginning to ask yourself if it's all worth it?"

"I fucked up guys," she blurts out. "I fucked up and I put the Kings in a damn near impossible situation. It worked out in the end but not without damage."

"Damage to you and Derri," Cael adds in. "But somehow the older King, Adam, is now married with his happily ever after?" he asks critically.

Sure, Cael didn't know a thing about what went down but his question still hit the nail on the head. Adam and Ariana still found each other and are living their well-deserved happy ending.

"Lass, Derri found you...he found his way back to you when half the *shite* in his memory went out the window," Cael reminds her.

"He has a point," Ben concurs.

"It's not him," she says beneath a breath. "It's me," she tells her friends.

She'd never think the day would come that she would witness in-sync eye-rolling from the two crime bosses. But that's exactly what happened.

"I don't know how to get us back to what we were. HE doesn't remember what we were. He loves me as I am now but I'm already *in*. This person that I am now is all he knows and it's who Derrick King wants at his side. I don't know if I can continue to be his queen and not fuck up..." *like I did and nearly lost everything.*

21

"Stop talking like there's two of them," Ben tells her with an added eye-roll and then leans back into his seat. "They're one and the same, Stella. They always have been. The monster, the husband, the guy you supposedly dated...they're all the same man. Just like who you are is one and the same."

"I agree with Gaston," Cael confesses. "*Ye* gotta stop separating everything. Compartmentalizing or whatever the *foock* it is *ye* do. Your life *is* what it is now, lass. *Ye* stumble, take the fall but get back up and move forward."

She sits quietly when the waitress comes over to take their order. So quietly and deep in thought that Ben orders her lunch for her.

"I hate you guys especially when you give me decent advice," she retorts with a smile. Everything that's been said is worth serious consideration.

Yet, she can't help but be unsure how to move forward...with her husband.

Seduction. That was her play and her best plan.

She can still see the burn and the longing in Derrick's eyes every time they connect with her own. Whatever the disconnection they may currently have, their physical need for each other has never dissolved.

That was made apparent at Adam's wedding when sparks flew every single time they got the chance to touch each other. She felt it to her soul and she can feel how much he wanted her permeating off of his tan skin. It rivaled her own need of him and the fire in his eyes said he knew it too.

The only problem was that she was never able to meet him eye to eye again. Not for long, at least. Not long enough for him to see how much guilt she was holding. Not long enough for the pain to settle upon her face. She'd laid hands on him and she knew no one has ever done that to Derrick King and lived to speak of it. She didn't even give him the chance to explain what could have happened. And she ripped her son from his father and home. It's a hard fucking pill to swallow. Especially after the year that they'd already had.

The cashier hands her credit card back along with the elegant bag full of brand new lingerie. "Thank you, Mrs. King," Brenda says with a smile.

She smiles in return and makes her way back to the car with Brooks trailing closely behind her. He seemed uncomfortable to follow her inside and she really didn't need him in there so he'd opted to stand guard in front of the store.

Brooks quickly gets into the driver's seat without asking. Probably because he'd been complaining about her driving the whole way here.

That's his new thing of late. Ever since he made amends with his past and accepted the love of a gorgeous soul like Pam, he's been less tense, happier, and more...*vocal* about his thoughts, about his plans...about *everything*.

She didn't mind though. He's still her most trusted. As much as she appreciated everything that Brooks has done for her so far, she prefers this version of him more because Rian gets to see the real Brooks too. She'd want nothing less for her son and the bond forming between the two important people in her life.

"How's it going with Miles and Sonia," she asks him as he maneuvers through traffic.

He grunts but she turns to see the smile on his face. "Put Miles in touch with Ronan for some real training if he really wants to keep fighting."

"Professionally though right? Not that underground shit," she asks.

"No doubt," he answers with a smirk. "Sonia is doing the whole beauty school gig."

"Cosmetology," she corrects him.

"Yeah...that shit," he mumbles. He sighs and they have a moment of quiet between them. "Thanks, Stell."

"For what?" she asks as she glances out of the window, watching cars and people pass by.

"All your help and support," he replies and then clears his throat a few times. "For buying a bum some lunch that day. For not turning your nose up like the snob I assumed you'd be."

"We both stepped foot into this together from the beginning, Tim. I wouldn't have lasted without you," she tells him her truth.

"I wouldn't have lived without you," he returns.

She grins at him and sticks out her tongue like a kid and he had the nerve to tousle her freshly done hair.

"You making moves?" he asks.

"Moves on what?"

His head nods to the back seat. "The lingerie. Getting your husband back," he says.

"Isn't it obvious?" she taunts.

"Bout time," he grumbles. "Hope it's obvious to him too. Man broods like a high school girl. I'm thinking the Twilight Saga would make a good gift for him this Christmas."

She full out laughs at him as he tries his best to hide his teeth from showing through his grin.

Brooks side-eyes her and all is lost. His booming laughter fills up the G-Wagon while he makes sure he's still driving safely through traffic.

Chapter
FOUR

It's been quite some time since he's been at the penthouse where Stella and his son have been living. Things needed to change and he needed to take matters into his own hands. Waiting for her to come to terms isn't working for him anymore. He doesn't know what's going on inside of her pretty little head and staying apart isn't going to help him figure that out either.

This distance is killing him. He doesn't know how much longer he can be without her.

One of her personal guards, James, is already at the door of the penthouse waiting for him when he steps off of the elevator. He nods at the man and James opens the door for him without question.

He can hear some commotion coming from the kitchen. It's Brooks and Rian doing whatever it is that they do. There is rustling and shuffling of items around in what sounds like a person digging for stuff and he doesn't pay it another second of his attention.

He heads toward Stella's room instead. Brooks and Rian can catch up to him once he says what he has to say to Stella. This isn't going to be a make-it-or-break-it conversation either. He's not giving her this choice anymore. She and Rian are coming home. End of discussion.

He can hear her speaking when he nears her bedroom door. "Stop that!" he hears her hiss.

He immediately stops his stride just next to the door. She's either not alone or she's on the phone with someone. The small gap in the door allows him to hear her crisp and clear. He also eyes the bag on the floor by the door. He'd know that bag anywhere. It's from her favorite lingerie boutique.

"It's too big," she gasps. "I can't do this," he hears her.

There's a low grumbling from someone, somewhere inside of that bedroom and his hands are balled into fists. This isn't fucking happening. This can't be the real reason for her resistance.

"Okay, okay," she hisses on the other side of that door. "But it's going to hurt."

Oh! Fuck NO! Hell fucking no. In the next instant, it's foot...meet door. That's exactly how he entered his cheating, estranged wife's bedroom.

The door clangs against the wall and then swings back toward him with a vengeance. He shoves it open in time to see Stella quickly pulling the covers off of the bed to cover the man laying on the floor.

She's on her knees wearing a robe and she better pray to God that she's not fucking naked beneath that robe.

"Derrick!" she gasps, her hands releasing the cover and then coming up to her chest in surprise. "I thought you were Brooks with Rian," she says.

"Are you fucking kidding me?!" he hollers back at her. "You brought a fucking bastard into your bed and you're afraid OUR son was going to coming into the room?"

He puts his hand on his holster. It trembles on the handle of the cool steel.

"What?" she asks, her brows nearly touching.

Stella looks from him and then down to the unmoving body on the floor. The fucking asshole was completely covered from head to toe with his pants down to his ankles. She looks back up at him afterward, shaking her head, a smile slowly crossing her face.

Is she serious? She thinks this is funny? Cuckholding him is no fucking joke.

"FUCK YOU!" he yells at her.

Instead of shooting the motherfucker dead, he turns his heel on a dime and walks the other fucking way. It's too fucking much. It's too much to stand there and watch her continue to laugh at him like the fucking fool she's clearly made him out to be. Their son is in the house while his mother is playing house with another man. Rian didn't need to see his shattered father commit murder either. That did need to be one of his precious son's first memories.

He reaches the door just as Brooks was coming out of the kitchen with a box in one hand and the other arm holding Rian.

"Hey," Brooks grunts at him.

Brooks was in on this too. That shouldn't be a surprise. He's Stella's guy after all. Fuck him too!

He reaches for Rian and plucks his son out of the man's arm. Brooks didn't even care to ask any questions but hurriedly continues to walk past him.

"Dada!" Rian squeals excitedly.

"That's right, baby boy. Daddy has you, son."

He exits the penthouse suite with a simple nod at James who doesn't stop to ask one single question. She's built quite the fucking team for herself, hasn't she? A team that keeps their mouth shut and their loyalty tight.

He brushes past Emilia and Aleksander when they get off the elevator, taking their newly vacated lift.

"Derrick!" Aleksander calls out to him.

He doesn't respond but jams his fingers on the buttons, closing the door behind him.

He's survived being lost in the jungle, fucking shot multiple times, and a goddamn car explosion in the past few years. None of that was as gut-wrenching or as painful as losing her.

Nothing.

Chapter
FIVE

"What the fuck just happened?" Peter mumbles to her once he weakly untangles the covers from over his face.

"I think I...*we*...just gave my husband the wrong impression," she replies.

She takes a look over herself in her robe. Depending on how long Derrick had been eavesdropping, yeah...he definitely had gotten the wrong impression.

"Here's the best we got," Brooks interrupts from behind her.

She turns around to see Brooks with a small first aid kit in his hand. "Where's Rian?" she asks.

"With his dad," Brooks replies. "I got this," he tells her next and then juts his chin at Peter on the ground. "You need to go get dressed. King didn't look too pleased."

Brooks settles on the floor next to Peter and throws the covers off. She's going to have to replace those covers for Ben since the bloodstains currently on it are probably not going to come off, even with the superior cleaning service provided here at the Mirabeau.

"Shit," Brooks hisses once he assesses the extremely deep gash on Peter's upper thigh.

"Artery?" Peter asks, his voice weak and woozy.

"You'd be dead by now if that's the case," Brooks replies. "This ain't gonna help," he says, tossing the small first aid kit onto the ground next to the sewing kit she'd abandoned by Peter's leg. Peter had seriously lost too much blood or was just plain crazy to think she'd be able to sew his wound shut.

"Emi is coming right?" Peter looks up and asks her. His eyes were starting to glaze over already.

She nods at him. "Any minute now. Just hang on."

Peter closes his eyes and exhales loudly. It's a good sign. He's still breathing. It'd take more than a five-inch slice to the thigh to kill the Russian Prince anyway.

She stares at the gape on his flesh and the amount of blood flowing over the side of his large upper thigh. She might have to reconsider that thought about him not dying by the slice. It's a deep wound and it's profusely bleeding.

She hurriedly heads to her dressing room to change out of her attire. Earlier, she'd just stepped out of the shower when Brooks and James had busted in through her bedroom door, half carrying Peter and then dropping him onto the floor. She'd been lucky to even have the robe on at that time.

"Rian doesn't need to see all this blood," Brooks had explained to her when she'd rushed out of the bathroom. He'd left her with James and Peter. She assumed he rushed back to Rian who she had left watching TV in the living room with Brooks before stepping into the shower.

Peter must have requested for James to call Emilia because James was already on the phone and speaking at that point.

And now...she had some explaining to do to Derrick.

On the one hand, it made her smile. Forget what Derrick King has told her about his lack of jealousy. There is NO lack of jealousy. Derrick has plenty of it. And it made her feel phenomenal that her husband still felt that way about her. It was only going to make her plan go more smoothly.

Emilia's screech pierces into her thoughts. She can hear Emilia anxiously speaking Russian and Aleksander was firing away questions as well.

She leaves her closet to meet them after she made sure she was more presentable.

"Stella," Emilia says to her. "This is more serious than I thought. James, he did not say it was this serious. I don't have enough here but to start an IV."

"I'll call our doctor," she tells Emilia. "Do the best you can to keep him alive until then." She grabs her phone and makes the call, requesting the doctor arrive immediately.

"Does anyone know what happened?" Aleksander saunters up and asks her once she hangs up with Dr. Heinz.

"No," she shakes her head. "Brooks and James dragged him in here and that was it. We called Emilia right away. Peter hasn't been able to say a single thing about what happened yet."

She steps past Aleks and begins dialing on her phone again. "Excuse me, Aleks. I need to make this call."

She steps into the hallway with the phone pressed to her ear.

"Ben," she says when her friend answers. "Something's happened at the hotel. Peter Ivanov showed up at the penthouse stabbed and he's losing a lot of blood."

"What?" Ben asks in astonishment.

"Yeah...exactly! Can you have your guys check how he got past everyone, which way he came, and what the hell happened to him? He's in and out right now and can't answer anything."

"Stell, do we really need to fucking dance with the Russians again?" Ben asks.

"I don't think we have a choice right now. He came to me and I happen to be at *your* place, dude. I think we just got an invite to prom."

"Fuck!" she hears Ben hiss. *"Yeah. I'll head down there and have my guys start working on it. Some motherfuckers are going to be looking for new jobs too."*

She hangs up after their conversation, seeking Brooks and Rian.

She finds Brooks in the living room on the phone. He must have heard her coming or smelled her. Whichever since she was sure her footsteps were lighter than a feather. He turns around and bells ring off in her head when she sees his anguished expression.

"Where's Rian?" she asks immediately.

He pockets his phone and fully turns around to face her.

"I handed him off to his dad, thinking he'd stay but King took off with him. He's not answering his phone. I called Pam already but if he's taking baby boy there, he won't be there for another twenty minutes."

She shouldn't be alarmed. Rian is with his dad and Derrick would never put their son in harm's way. But something sparks her to hurriedly dial Derrick's phone number anyway. With their relationship hanging on by a thread and this misunderstanding, who knows what could be running through his mind.

Her call goes straight to voicemail.

"I'll just go to the estate," she tells Brooks. "I'll pick Rian up."

Brooks shakes his head.

"No?" she asks. "Why not?"

"We need to make sure it's safe first. Don't know what's going on with Ivanov or if we're going to catch that heat. I don't want you walking out the door right now. Let King keep baby boy safe for now."

He's right. She nods at him. He's right. Besides, it might give Derrick some time to cool off before she can explain anything to him.

She didn't have another minute to object or derive a better plan because James was showing Dr. Heinz in and directing the doctor toward her bedroom.

James stops to speak to her and Brooks, allowing the doctor to go on ahead. "Jason's down with the security team going over the cams," James informs them. "I've gotta be out front. It's only me and you Brooks."

Brooks nods to James and then turns to face her. "Stell, get your piece and have it ready. James will take one end. I'll be out front by the door. If Aleks isn't helping his sister and the doc, might be worthwhile to have him armed too. Just in case."

"Yeah," she replies. "Ben's coming over. I'm sure he's bringing more of his men. I'm going to call Adam at the estate and give them a heads up."

Chapter
SIX

Instead of parking the car in front of the mansion, he opted for the garage. He's in no mood to speak to anyone and he's sure there would be questions if he brought Rian in through the front door without his mother nor any of the baby's personal merci-nannies. It would look odd to anyone for him to walk inside with the baby and not have a baby bag or even a blanket.

Luckily, no one even saw him using the back staircase up to his wing of the mansion. It's fucking hilarious how the world still turns while his has just about crumbled to the fucking ground. At least he still has Rian. No way in fucking hell is he going to give his son up.

Rian squeals when he enters the nursery. The baby has already begun recognizing his room and choosing his favorite toys.

"Home, Dada!" Rian exclaims with both fists pumped above his head.

"That's right, son. You're home. First things first. Bath. Because you're not smelling cute at all right now."

He can't help but chuckle at Rian's little pout. Rian must think it's a conundrum. To have to choose between playing with his favorite toys or taking a warm bath which his son equally loves. If only life remained that simple.

For the next couple of hours, he'd spent time out of his head and focusing only on his son. Bathing him, reading to him, chasing him around the nursery, and then finally putting him down for a nap.

It was at that time that his heart truly began to break.

He leans against Rian's wall and sinks down onto his ass, watching the rise and fall of his son's chest. Wondering how Rian is going to be affected by everything. Stella can go fuck herself if she thinks she's going to be taking Rian with her. To be raised by another man. That's not going to fucking happen. No matter how much he loved her. He loves his son even more than that and he's given her enough.

No...he'd given her everything. All of him. And it *wasn't* enough.

To think that he'd gone over there to demand that she come home. And if that didn't work, he'd been ready to grovel. She probably would have shut the door on him and then laughed behind his back before going back to fuck whoever she was fucking.

Fuck! The thought of some other man touching her, kissing her, being inside of her is tearing him up from the inside out. The thoughts are like a virus quickly spreading and burning every cell in his body. How did they fall so fucking far?

How did HE fall so fucking far?

He'd kept all aspects of his life cutthroat for this very reason. Because he knew how much love can destroy. His mother's love and faith for his father literally became the death of her. His father's own regrets were essentially what led to his own demise.

Love made people fucking miserable. He'd witness it time and time again watching business associates fuck over their wives and families a hundred times over. He'd steered clear of it...until Stella. Now, misery has arrived at his doorstep with a red fucking bow. Just in time for the holidays.

Oh, it's a wonderful life alright.

He'd sat inside his son's room with his thoughts churning well past nightfall when he saw movement on the security camera. Stella and Brooks pulled right up to the front of the mansion. It fucking infuriated him that it took her *this* fucking long to show up for their son.

He quietly leaves Rian asleep in his room with the nursery's door open. If Rian wakes, someone will hear him if he isn't back yet.

He can hear her muffled voice speaking to Adam and Ariana when he reaches the grand staircase. He rolls his neck to loosen the corded muscles and slips the mask on. Stella has always been his weakness, seeing through him when no one else could. She won't be today and if she does, then she should be very afraid.

"Derrick!" she exclaims when their eyes meet.

"You've been home this whole time?" Adam asks him incredulously. "Why the fuck haven't you answered your phone?"

"Left it in the car," he mumbles when he stops next to Adam.

"Oh, thank God!" Stella says, looking relieved. She looks him up and down and then just past him as if searching for something. "Where's Rian? He's okay right?"

"Why wouldn't he be?" he growls. "He's probably too young to be traumatized by watching his mother fucking another man anyway."

"DERRICK!" she screams at him in astonishment. Her eyes grow as wide as saucers.

"Woah! What the hell are you talking about?" Adam says, stepping up to him.

"There's been a misunderstanding," Stella says to everyone.

Brooks steps closer to his boss. Smart guy. Because the man might actually have to pry his hands from around Stella's slender neck to stop him from choking the life out of her.

"You're not taking him," he tells her as calmly as possible.

He doesn't give one fuck about what she has to say about his *misunderstanding*. She's not going to smooth talk her way out of this, especially when the prize is their son. Bat her fucking eyes all she wants. It's not happening.

"Excuse me?" she gasps. Her cheeks flushing a shade of pink he can't remember ever seeing.

She takes a step closer to him. Her fragrant both attacks and soothes him at the same time. And for the first time, they are face to face. Eye to eye. Sparks are flying between the two of them. Flying and flaming, ready to burn everything to the fucking ground.

Her eyes sear into him furiously. Her nostrils flare in anger. Her lips press thinly together but she doesn't say anything. Merely trying to murder him with her gaze alone.

"You want to fuck someone else, go right ahead, Stellina. My son stays home from now on," he tells her. His tone is clipped. It's cut and dry and deadly serious.

"Woah, Woah! What the hell is going on, brother?" Adam asks, stepping in between him and Stella. "You haven't even heard what she has to say and you really should. It's not what you think and you need to—"

It's Stella who pushes Adam out of the way, cutting Adam off. Then she steps up to where his brother was standing.

Ariana reaches for Adam's arm, pulling him back quietly.

"Is that what you think of me? It's that how you see me, Derrick?" Stella hisses at him.

"I saw what I saw," he replies through gritted teeth.

"And I saw what I saw many fucking times, Derrick," she hisses back at him. Her anger and venom unhinged. "Each one of *your* misunderstandings was forgiven."

"Oh, were they now, wife?" he asks sarcastically. "That would only mean that the *misunderstanding* that *you* helped create was only an excuse for you to not have to come home, doesn't it? Not because of anything I did. Things are becoming quite clear now, Stella."

It's the first time he's ever placed blame on her for the events that nearly led Adam to have to marry a fucking bitch like Isabella Romano. That same event tore his own marriage apart though. It doesn't fucking matter at this moment if he really blamed her or not. Hurt people...*hurt* people. And that's what he wanted to do. It's petty as fuck. But he's trembling, needing to do something. Anything to ease the burn.

"Derrick!" Adam barks at him.

Stella takes a step back into Brooks. His words stung her.

"So, you can finally tell me the truth now, huh?" she asks. She looks back and forth between him and Adam. "Is that how you all feel?"

Good! Let it hurt just as much as she'd hurt him.

"Of course not!" Adam exclaims.

He, on the other hand, doesn't budge. He had to hold his ground or he'd be losing his son.

Stella falters but for that second though. He can see the moment the fire returns to her. In full force. She takes a step toward him, her face flushed with fury, and Brooks steps up right behind her.

"My son comes with me," she demands, her hands balled into cute tiny fists.

Even with the traumatic brain injury, he'd learn and knew of all her tells. The way she's standing, the way she's speaking, the way she's furiously eye-murdering him where he stands. This isn't his little star that he's speaking to. This is Stella King that he's ready to go to war with. She's a fucking formidable foe too.

"Over my dead body," he snarls back at her.

42

The moment he steps closer, he hears Brooks drawing his gun.

His hand immediately goes to his holster and unclips his own weapon as well. Stella's eyes land where his hand rests on the Glock.

"Are you sure you want this to go down this way, Derrick?" she asks him calmly yet with nothing but ice in her voice.

She's anything but calm though. He can tell by how heavy her breathing has gotten. He can see the rapid rising and falling of her lovely fucking chest. Her eyes are void of the compassion that comes naturally to her and her whole body seems to be flushed a darker shade of pink at this point.

"It's not going down with you walking out here with my son today, Stella," he warns.

She looks at Adam and then nods at Ariana.

He doesn't take his eyes off of her for a second.

Stella takes a step back, her whole body stiffening. "I *will* be back for my son, King. I promise you. When I do, it might be the last time you see him. So tuck him into bed gently at night, kiss him every moment you can, and breathe in his smell as much as your lungs will let you. It might be your last time breathing."

Such beauty. Such fire and heat. His little star isn't fucking around and she glows with wrath.

With her promise, she turns on her heel and shoves past Brooks.

He watches her short and tight body quickly walking the fuck out of his life. That's how a war just started. The war between husband and wife. King versus King.

43

Chapter
SEVEN

The echo of her retreat still resonates through him when Adam's hysterical laugh pierces through his misery.

"I'm glad you're so damn entertained," he growls at Adam.

"You're a fucking idiot of the worst kind, brother."

He looks at his brother and takes the step up, hands balled again. Too much tension and frustration. He needed to blow off steam for a long time now and he's sure Adam can handle the blowout. But Adam walks away, pacing with his head tossed back into a full-blown belly laugh as if he's lost his fucking mind.

"Derrick," Ariana says to him with a loud sigh. "You shouldn't have done that. You should have listened," she says quietly.

He glares at her. His little mouse of a sister-in-law. To his surprise, she doesn't flinch nor withdrawals like he'd expected her to.

45

No. She stands solid, face to face with him for the first time since they'd met. What the fuck is it with these King women? They've all lost their fucking minds and have forgotten who's running the show.

"She was coming home," Ariana tells him. "She came here to make sure Rian was okay and to say that she was coming home."

"What?" he asks incredulously, staring at her as if she'd sprouted a second head.

"She called Adam about a misunderstanding. She came to explain and to say that she was coming home because things were happening that she didn't want to be a part of," Ariana repeats.

"You didn't see what I saw, Ariana. If she was coming home, it's only because she knew she was caught. I've had Rian for half the day before she showed up here looking for him. I don't even want to fucking think what she was doing during that time."

He didn't want to think about it but his mind had veered in that direction too many fucking times already.

Ariana shakes her head at him with exasperation when Adam returns to her side.

"She's given you chance after chance after all of your fuck-ups, brother. She's NEVER done anything to make you question her loyalty or her fidelity. Not once! She made a decision that affected the whole family and she was carrying that burden. At the first fucking chance that YOU were given to show her where she truly stood in this family, you fucking pounced on her!"

"What the fuck are you talking about?!" he hollers at Adam.

"The fucking guy on the floor wasn't someone she was fucking. It was Peter Ivanov—"

46

"ARE YOU FUCKING KIDDING ME?!" he cuts Adam off. Of all fucking people! She's fucking Ivanov.

"Shut up, you fucking cow! Shut up and listen!" Adam yells at him. His brother plants his hands on his hips and takes a deep breath to calm himself down.

"Peter Ivanov was nearly stabbed to death while on his way to visit Stella. He was stabbed inside the fucking elevator on the way up to *her* floor and whoever did the deed escaped through the elevator's escape hatch. She was only trying to cover him up because he was bloody as fuck and she didn't want Rian to see that!"

"You really should have heard her out first," Ariana adds softly.

His jaw hit the ground with a loud bang that echoed through every fucking square foot of the mansion. He can literally feel the dunce hat sprouting on top of his hollow head.

Oh, fuck. OH. FUCK.

"Oh, fuck," he gasps.

"You've just declared war on her when she's been trying to reach you all fucking day. The penthouse isn't safe for her while Peter has to stay there until he can be moved. She was coming home, you asshole! And now? You just sent her right the fuck back there," Adam tells him, face flushed as red as the poinsettias spread out through the mansion.

"Your phone," he hastily asks his brother since his is still in the car.

Adam pulls his phone out from his pocket and dials then holds it up to his ear.

"Straight to voicemail," Adam tells him not even five seconds later.

"Shit," he says. "Shit!"

"Give her some space to calm down. You said a harsh thing, Derrick." It's Ariana that speaks to him this time.

Adam turns and faces him. "She'd been feeling guilty and isolated before this and now she's probably feeling completely alone, Derrick. She's going to think we're all on YOUR side on this. She's going to believe we all hold her responsible for what fucking happened."

"I fucking know!" he howls out in frustration. "I only said it because I knew it would hurt her. It would fucking pierce her the way she fucking burned me seeing her half-naked on her knees next to another man! I didn't fucking mean it. Why the fuck didn't you stop me?!"

"As if Derrick King would let anyone step in front of him!" Adam yells back, getting into his face. "As if you were going to let anyone else get a word in during the Derrick King show."

"Hey! Calm down, Adam." Ariana gets in between him and his brother this time.

"I should follow her," he thinks out loud.

"Do you know not your own wife?" Adam hisses, his hand shooting out in the direction that Stella had just made her exit. "She'll shoot on the fucking spot. You were in Derrick King mode with her and she's going to think you're coming for her. This is as bad as it's going to get."

"I agree," Ariana adds in again. "Give her at least one night to cool off."

He lets out a loud sigh of frustration and turns around to find Claire walking down the stairs with Rian in her arms.

"I'm sorry," Claire says nervously. "I heard him crying and changed him."

"It's fine," Ariana tells Claire and proceeds to take the baby into her arms. Rian snuggles into his aunt's chest and suckles on his thumb, falling back asleep.

"Ariana," he says softly so as not to wake Rian. "Do you mind having him stay with you tonight?" he asks.

"Of course not," Ariana replies with a warm smile.

"And what do you plan on fucking up next?" Adam lowly growls at him.

"I have to do *something...anything!*" he tells his brother.

Chapter
EIGHT

"There's a lot of movement here, Adam. It's heavily guarded right now by Gaston's and Ivanov's crews but I want some of our own men here. Sully and Tommy are with me now but with this many people on guard, something serious must be happening," he says into the phone to his brother.

He eyes the hotel that Stella has been living in again. The men on guard duty are indistinguishable by the everyday passersby but he knew who they were. Some of them had obvious ink and then others, he just knew from having seen them around or the way they cautiously moved from left to right. He'd watched them study just about everyone that came and left the Mirabeau.

"I'll reach out to Gaston and coordinate," Adam tells him into the phone. *"At least Rian isn't there right now."*

He hangs up without another word after that.

He might have started a war with Stella but now that he sees all this precarious movement, he isn't one bit sorry for taking Rian home. It's been two days with this being the third night that he's been sitting here in the car. Neither Stella nor Ivanov has been seen. Not even Brooks and her two other guards have left. That's no surprise. They go where she goes. The only person coming and going has been Ben Gaston.

"Let me go in," Tommy says from the front seat. "She should be calm by now and I can get information or ask her if she needs anything at all."

"He's right, Boss," Sully adds in from the driver's seat. "We need info. It might be none of our business but Stella's in there."

He mulls it over for a bit before deciding to go along with it. "Go ahead," he tells Tommy.

"Where the fuck are our men?" Sully mutters from the front seat.

"Adam!" he yells into the phone. "I sent Tommy inside over an hour ago and I haven't heard back from him since. Where are our men?"

"They should be there by now," Adam replies sounding perplexed. *"I spoke with Gaston himself and made sure he was aware."*

52

"Fuck this!" he growls into the phone.

"*Stay put! Don't fucking go in there without knowing what you're walking into!*" Adam yells as he hangs up the phone, dismissing whatever else Adam was saying.

"You sure, Boss?"

He eyes Sully through the rearview mirror and nods.

"Shit," Sully whispers before reaching into the center console and pulling out two Glocks. Sully checks the mags on both guns and then hands one of the Glocks over to him.

He tucks the piece nicely behind his back and then checks the Glock safely tucked in his holster. He lets out a loud exhale and reaches for his suit jacket then checks the time on his Rolex. It's just past seven.

"We're going in as casual as possible like I'm here to visit my wife. Nothing more. If the place is being watched, it'll play out smoothly since I'll only have you with me and no backup."

"Smoothly," Sully repeats with a chuckle. "Shit never goes smoothly."

"Tell me about it," he hisses as he opens his door and steps out anxiously. He'd even forgotten to let Sully step out and open the door for him.

He can feel eyes on him as he and Sully walk up to the entrance of the hotel. It prickles at his nerve ends. He doesn't let the feeling bother him since they are most likely bratva or Gaston's men. Both crews are there to keep an eye on their bosses. Hopefully, Kings' men are mingled in and watching his back too.

Inside the lobby, things are eerily quiet. People are walking about but mostly it's the hotel's staff members in uniform and not the usual hustle and bustle of the holiday crowd of visitors to Clandon City. With Christmas approaching next week and the Mirabeau being a prime shopping center, it should be busier.

"Something's off," Sully whispers from behind him as they wait for the elevator.

He laughs nonchalantly, mostly for show. "Everything's off," he adds.

The elevator dings and he steps into the empty box while Sully jams on the button to the penthouse floor. When the door closes, he moves back, remembering not to stand underneath the escape hatch since that's how Ivanov's attacker allegedly escaped.

He eyes the numbers that light up every time they reach the next level. He manages to stop himself from fidgeting while he tries to breathe some patience into his rabid thoughts.

On the eighteenth floor, just one floor before the penthouse floor, the elevator stops with a hard jolt.

"What the fuck?" Sully grumbles as he jams on the buttons.

They lose power seconds afterward.

"Fuck!" he gasps.

Chapter
NINE

"What's going on?!" she asks Brooks when he bursts through the front door of the penthouse. She tries to keep the draft from blowing out the candle she has lit by shielding it with one hand.

"I don't know but it seems the whole building has lost power. Not just this floor. And the backup lights should have come on by now," Brooks replies. "Be ready for anything, Stella." He hands her a small flashlight. "I'm going to my room to grab another one."

She nods at him then puts the candle in her hand on top of the coffee table. "I'll let Peter and Emilia know."

She dials Ben as she heads to the bedroom, *her* bedroom, that Peter has been recovering in. He's getting stronger by the day but Emilia wasn't confident enough for him to move back to their own turf yet. Especially when Peter's attacker is still on the loose and with little detail on that person.

"I have people working on it already," Ben says into the phone as soon as he answers her call. *"The place is like a fortress, Stell. Stay put. I'm on my way anyway."*

"Thanks, Ben." She hangs up and then steps into the bedroom.

Emilia is huddled next to a sleeping Peter. Aleks was sitting with his legs bouncing next to the bed with the light from his phone lighting the space.

"Just a power outage," she informs the siblings. "The wind must be stronger than we thought. A storm is probably coming. We always get one around this time of year."

Aleks smiles at her, seemingly calmer now. "Storms? *Nyet.* Americans know nothing of winter storms until you have lived through *russkaya metel'*, Stella." He laughs quietly afterward.

"I have no clue what you just said there," she tells him with a smile. But everything inside is twisted. Something's off. She can feel it and she's learned very quickly that the key to surviving this game is to trust your gut.

"*Russkaya metel'* is a Russian blizzard," Peter informs her from the bed. "It's equivalent to what you Americans call a nor'easter but ten times worse."

"Maybe twenty times worse," Aleks says. "AND we would still have to get to school!"

"Well, thank God for snow days!" she teases.

"Soft Americans," Peter mumbles with a smile followed by a yawn. His brows furrow closely together after he settles.

56

"What is it?" Emilia asks her brother.

"Shh...," Peter replies with a finger to his lips.

"It's already quiet," she says to him.

"Exactly," Peter says into the room. He moves to a sitting position, reaching for a shirt to throw on.

Brooks steps inside now too and she looks him up and down. "Any word?" she asks.

He shakes his head at her and then looks over to Peter. "Can you move?" he asks Peter.

Brooks's question snaps her into action. Peter's right. It's already quiet. Too quiet when the hotel should be bustling with employees scrambling to restore power for their guests.

She moves to the window to see if she can see any movement down below. The penthouse has a magnificent view of the city but it's also strategically located right above the back of the hotel where you can watch deliveries and movement going in and out of the building. But tonight...it's dead. There's no movement outside except for the swaying trees and there should be.

"Let's go," Peter says. Peter is fully dressed and on his feet with both Emilia's and Aleksander's help.

"We should stay and wait for Ben," she suggests.

Peter scoffs unabashedly.

"Hey!" she scowls. "He's put you up this long."

"He also couldn't find the motherfucker that did this to me either, *ptichka*."

He has a point. A pretty odd and rare point because Ben is usually on top of his game especially when it comes to the security of one of his legit businesses. The Mirabeau is his pride and joy even over The Fields and he would have made it a priority to find something.

If he hasn't, that means something is going down.

"Let's move," Brooks urges.

With flashlights lighting the way, they steadily exit the penthouse. James and Jason are both waiting right outside of the doorway by the stairwell. Of course, the elevators are most likely not working without power.

"Dead quiet," Peter mumbles.

Jason leads everyone down the flight of steps. She watches Peter wincing with every step on his injured leg even with the help of his siblings crutching his weight.

They reach the next floor below and Jason nearly walked into the heavy door when he shoves on the bar and the door doesn't budge.

"It's locked?" James asked incredulously. "That's a fire hazard. There should be people moving in and out of this doorway by now."

"Did they do an evacuation?" Emilia asks.

She shakes her head. They would have known. Ben would have told her if that were the case.

"This floor is for the luxury suites," Brooks says calmly. "Maybe there weren't any guests."

She looks at him as if he's gone dumb. "Really?" she asks. "It's the holidays. This place would have been completely booked this time of year."

"Wait here," James tells everyone. "I'm going to scout the levels below first"

He takes off without further instruction and they wait for his return. The whole time, she can feel more goosebumps rising. The only footsteps audible had to be James. The light from his flashlight growing dimmer and dimmer with each passing second.

"Where is everyone?" she murmurs more to herself than anyone.

"No signal," Brooks sets as he checks his phone.

The stairwell grows darker when Brooks pockets his phone. The only light surrounding them now is the one coming from the flashlight she's holding in her hand and from Aleksander's phone.

Both she and Peter check their phones at the same time as well. She shakes her head at Peter and he returns the gesture.

"What the fuck is happening?" Peter growls. "No power? No phone? Locked doors? No people!"

"Mm...maybe it is the storm," Aleks answers nervously. "Maybe it knocked out some tower close by?"

"It's possible," Brooks says. He steps to the door and looks through the small window before grimly stepping back.

Rian. Thank God the baby isn't here. She misses him down to her soul but he's safe...with his dad.

Derrick. Damn! What a shit show their last meeting turned out to be.

She'd always felt that deep down, the Kings blamed her for what happened, for her grandfather trying to force her hand into returning to his side by using them. It was one of the reasons that she'd teeter-tottered about going back to Derrick's side without a plan in place to prevent that from ever happening again. She'd found solace by reminding herself that Adam ended up with Ariana, his love...his wife anyway.

Derrick took that tiny bit of solace away from her when he said that their marriage is in shambles because of *her* decisions. He'd blamed her. Whether he said it to shield himself from the hurt that he must have been feeling or not, it had stung and it had stuck.

All she'd ever wanted was to be with Derrick. She'd moved heaven and earth to make it happen. But with every step forward, there were three setbacks. This dance is getting old. Derrick was the fuel that controlled the burning flame. Without him, everything would just burn to the ground.

Karma. That's the word that comes to mind.

She'd burned Isabella Romano until there weren't even ashes left for nothing more than revenge. It didn't fix her marriage. It didn't do anything other than tip the scales further for her descent to hell.

Maybe she's already arrived at her own Hell. One without Derrick King.

Derrick basically shoved her out the door and now he has Rian. He isn't going to let go of her son without a fight...without a war. Putting his hand on his weapon showed her just how serious he was.

"Our coms aren't working either," Jason says while he taps on the earpiece nestled in his ear.

This can't be a storm. Something is happening.

She reaches for the gun behind her back. "Shit," she hisses.

"What?" Brooks asks immediately.

"I forgot my gun, Brooks. I left it on the counter," she says with frustration. Her mind is all over the fucking place lately.

"Blade?" Brooks asks her.

She shakes her head. The only time she carried the blade was when she went out on business and the last time that happened was a long time ago. She didn't want to have it on her when she had Rian in her arms.

"Let's hope we won't need it, *dah*?" Emilia says.

A loud whistle pierces through the dimness, echoing off the metal rails and bouncing off the cement walls. A light flashes multiple times and Brooks moves past her to peer over the rails.

"It's James," he says. "We need to head down."

The trek down was slow and steady. Apprehension coils tighter with each passing level that they clear. Doors were locked and they haven't seen a single person yet. Nineteen floors of hotel rooms. It's impossible not to come across any other guests or employees. And if an evacuation had taken place, then Ben would have told her.

Chapter
TEN

"Peter, do you need to stop?" she asks once they reach James in the stairwell landing on the fifth floor.

Peter takes a moment and catches his breath before answering. "I'm okay," he says following a deep breath. "Stitches are still intact."

"This is the first unlocked door I came to," James informs everyone. "The one beneath is locked so I came back here. Already scoped the whole floor and it seems safe but I don't want to take chances as we move through."

"What's the plan?" she asks James.

"We clear the floor and see if we can get to the other set of stairs. Maybe more luck with those," James replies.

"It's the only solid that we have right now, Stella," Brooks says with a nod.

"I agree," Jason concurs and opens the door, taking point.

She follows him with Aleks next to her. James has fallen back to help Emilia with Peter now and Brooks is on everyone's six. The floor is completely covered in darkness. The only thing she sees is the red Exit lights. Probably because they are on backup batteries.

"It's been too long for the generators not to have kicked in by now," she says with her hand on Jason's back.

That's how they've trained through scenarios like this. With her unarmed, the best way for them to protect her is for her to completely trust each of them. Her hand on him tells him where she is at all times without him having to spare a second to look back. She moves only when he moves.

"Check!" Jason calls out.

"What?" Aleks asks from next to her.

"He's telling the others that we're at the halfway mark of the floor," she replies.

She reaches for Aleks's hand and pulls him closer. He clings on and she gives his hand a squeeze. It's deja vu all over again. This time with a young man, not a teenage boy, since Aleksander Ivanov hit a growth spurt in just under a year. The gentle boy now seems hardened, not just physically, but he's very much coming into the Bratva prince that he was born to become.

The sound of Jason clearing his throat and his jerking body snaps her out of memory lane.

"What's wrong?" she asks.

Then it hits her. It started with an itchy tingle in the back of her throat. One that she can't seem to clear no matter how much saliva she swallows or tries to. Aleks is doing the same thing and making grunting noises from next to her too.

"It's gas!" Jason cries out. "Try to cover your noses!" He pulls his neck gaiter over his nose and moves quickly now.

"Go! Go!" Brooks hollers from behind their group.

She feels Jason moving faster. Someone is also behind her, pushing her to move just as quickly but it's getting harder and harder to be able to breathe without the feeling of fire ants gnawing her esophagus.

"Almost to the door!" Jason yells.

She drops her hand from covering her nose and sprints to keep up with Jason as they approach the red Exit sign toward the end of the hallway.

The burning in her throat feels like razors at this point, ripping and shredding her flesh from the inside out. She coughs excessively enough for tears to spill. Her tears are what keeps her vision clear as the hallway now begins to fill with fog or was it more of the godforsaken pepper gas that's trying to stop her from breathing.

She falls to her knees.

Aleks drops right next to her.

The smoke and fog were so thick now that she can't be sure if anyone is still left standing. All she can hear are the sounds of puttering and coughing.

Then...everything seems to light up like the Christmas tree in the town square.

"Flashbang!" she hears someone yell through the ringing in her ears.

Chapter
ELEVEN

"You promised...you'll always find me."

It's those words that slowly wake him; not the ringing in his ear nor the pounding in his head. It's the feeling inside his soul that Stella needs him. Their connection won't allow him to ignore that no matter how at odds they are with each other.

He sits up slowly through the throbbing in the back of his head. His eyes are wide open and even when he's sure his vision is sharp again, it's complete darkness.

What the fuck happened?

"Sully," he calls out into the dark, remembering who'd been with him.

He listens and waits. Waits for a response. A sound. The sound of Sully's breathing. Anything. But he's alone. The only sound he can hear is the one coming from him.

He and Sully had waited a good ten minutes for the back-up generators or the power to come back on. Of course, neither did. He and Sully had to pry the elevator doors open with brute force and sheer will alone. At least they hadn't been stuck between floors.

They'd navigated the whole floor and didn't see another soul, only coming across one open door to a set of stairwells.

"Why does it feel like we're sheep being herded?" Sully had mumbled to him.

He couldn't disagree with Sully either. They weren't herded very far though. Doors were locked and they'd never come across anyone either.

They'd just walked onto the fourth floor through the door from the stairwell when they were immediately assaulted with some sort of gas. Sully had tried to push him back through the door that they came through but he'd seen shadows and figures approaching them. Sully goes down to his knees first. He'd thought that the gas was what did Sully in but he'd stared into the mask-covered face of someone in heavy tactical gear and a rifle in his hand. It was the last thing he can remember.

Now he's awake and alone in the dark. "Fuck," he mumbles.

He gets to his knees and then onto his feet, checking his pockets. His phone and his guns are gone. He seems to be intact for the most part except for the splitting headache at the back of his head.

He slowly stretches his arms out, trying to feel for anything solid to figure out where the fuck he is. There's carpet beneath his feet. He'd felt it when he'd first woken up. The room isn't cold either. It's actually almost room temperature which isn't usually a necessity granted for hostages if indeed he is one.

His palm rubs against a wall. He can feel grooves on the wall too. Wallpaper. It had to be. It took him only ten steps to get from where he was to the wall so the room wasn't a big one.

He had to still be in the hotel. But separated from Sully.

What the fuck is going on? Things have been extremely calm and quiet in their city especially with this alliance with Gaston and McCullen. Now he wonders if the time has finally come to dissolve this alliance. Is this Gaston making a play? Especially with McCullen visiting Ireland for the holidays.

Can this be Stella building her own Army against him? He'd pissed her off enough to make sure that it was a possibility. Gaston and McCullen would back Stella up in a heartbeat. Those fucking bastards.

He continues to feel his way along the wall in the dark. He'd gone into a closet. He'd found the bathroom and left his fingerprints all over a fucking mirror. He'd found the door locked. And yes, he'd tried to kick it down. It didn't budge. He'd even found something else interesting. No fucking windows for him to draw the curtains back for any kind of lighting.

He takes a deep breath in frustration and immediately her scent awakens all of his senses. Her scent, her sweet voice, has pulled

69

him out of the depths of hell and back to her one too many times. He'd recognize it anywhere.

"Stella?" he calls out quietly.

She doesn't answer but he knows she's close...unless she had a hand in putting him in this fucking room. There's always that.

But he can feel it in his gut, just like he did when he'd woken up with no memory of her. His every cell is urgently screaming that he needed to find her; to find his missing half. Stella needs him. That's something he has to hold on to for now.

"Baby," he calls out again as he stumbles around the dark.

Still no answer.

Instead of scouring the walls, he focuses on the side of the room that he'd caught wind of the floral scent of her perfume like an anxious search and rescue dog. When it gets stronger he knows he's close. He's never been in any of the rooms at the Mirabeau before except for the penthouse suite but he can almost be sure that he's in a room with one of those adjourning doors.

Thanks to the modern style that the Mirabeau has recently adapted, it took him several minutes to find a small groove in the wall. He pushes his fingertip in the notch and slides the door all the way with a loud bang and stands still assuming that his eyes would need to adjust to any kind of lighting but the door opens to yet another room shrouded in pitch black.

But he can feel her.

If she can find him and love him in the deepest and darkest part of him, finding her in a dark room should be like taking candy from a kid.

He feels his way along the wall again. Slowly, in case she's on the floor like he had been. It took him a few steps before his knee hits something. A bed.

He leans down, placing one knee on it.

"Stella," he calls out quietly, his hand sweeping from left to right until his fingers brush over her flesh. It had to be her.

His palm traces the open flesh up to her shoulders. She's cool to the touch but not cold which means she's not dead. Thank God.

"Stella. Baby," he calls out with a gentle shake.

Stella isn't normally a heavy sleeper. She was used to getting up in the middle of the night every time she'd heard Rian squeak through the baby monitor. She had to be drugged for her not to have heard the slamming of that door. Shit! Hopefully, she wasn't knocked in the back of the head as he had been. A concussion can be fucking bad right now, especially since he didn't know how long she'd been out.

He feels her slightly move and lets out the breath he didn't know he was holding.

"Baby," he whispers so as not to startle her.

"Derrick?" she replies in her sleepy voice. A sleepy voice he hasn't heard in too fucking long.

Chapter
TWELVE

In the dark, he hears her taking a deep breath as she tries to sit up on the bed but it's followed by her coughing and sputtering, gasping for air. There was nothing he could do to help her. He highly doubts that they'd be provided water for the occasion.

"D—Derrick?" she stutters out.

"I'm here. It's me," he replies, slowly rubbing her back up and down. "I'm sorry. I don't think there's anything for you to drink."

It takes her more than a few moments before she can breathe normally again. He pulls her into his arms, embracing her as close as possible. If some motherfucker was lurking in the dark and waiting to take them out, then he'd shield her from as much pain as his body could handle. It's been too fucking long since he'd held her and danger shouldn't be the thing that keeps bringing them back together.

73

"Why are you here? Where's Rian? Is he okay?" she asks in a rush, with her face pressed against his chest. "Please don't tell me he's been taken again."

"He should be at the mansion with Adam," he tells her.

"You—you didn't bring him with you?" she asks.

"No, Stella. He's safe. Our son is safe." God, he fucking hopes that the truth.

"Where are we?" she asks, pulling away from him much too soon.

He needed more. He'd missed her too much. Too much bullshit has come between them and this is the closest he's gotten to her.

He clears his throat before he speaks. "I think we're at the Mirabeau."

"The Mirabeau," she repeats. "There was a power outage and...and we were moving everyone down the stairs but doors were locked," she whispers. "I think we were knocked out by some kind of gas or something."

He can feel her twisting and turning but can't see what she's doing.

"There's no one else here. I woke up in the room next to this one," he tells her.

"Woke up?" she asks. "You...you got gassed too?"

"No. I got knocked upside the head," he tells her with a chuckle. Relieved that she didn't receive the same treatment.

"Oh my god! Are...are you okay? Your head...is it okay?" she asks.

She shifts on the bed, coming closer. Her hand slowly creeps over his chest, up over his throat, and then rests upon his cheek tenderly.

He covers her hand with his own before bringing it to his lips. "I'm okay. I didn't forget you," he tells her. If only he can see her. If only he can visually make sure that she's okay and intact. If only he can kiss her.

His dick decides to push up against the zipper at that moment because he has no concept of clear and present danger. He shifts to make sure Stella can't come closer. There are more pressing matters at hand. He'll be sure to fuck his wife seven days straight when they make it out of this...together.

"James. Jason. Brooks. The Ivanovs were with me too," she tells him.

He shakes his head even though she can't see him in the dark. "I haven't come across anyone yet."

"We didn't either when we moved through the floors. It was like moving through an abandoned building. It's Christmas time, this place should be packed."

"I know," he tells her. "Sully and I didn't come across anyone else either. Not even Tommy who I sent in an hour before we decided to follow him. Did he get to you?"

"No," she whispers. "Why were you here?"

"For you, Stella. I came here for you." There was no other answer.

"Derrick—"

"Baby, I'm sorry," he cuts her off. "I fucking overreacted. I—I lost my fucking shit when I shouldn't have. You have NEVER given me any reason to believe you'd do that to me. I fucked up. I really fucked up and I came here to grovel if I needed to."

"You threatened me," she whispers as she loosens her grip on his hand.

He tightens his grip over hers, stopping her from pulling away. "And you weren't the least bit scared," he replies.

"No, I wasn't. Not when it's for my son."

"*Our* son, Stella. And I shouldn't have said what I said. I didn't mean it. I don't blame you. Kings don't blame you, Stella. We don't but I wanted to hurt you because I'm petty as fuck and I thought you—"

She pinches his hand to stop him from speaking. "I know, Derrick. I know we need to talk but let's get out of here first and figure out what's going on. We have a son waiting for us."

"You're not going to run again, are you? Because I'll make sure you stay put in this fucking room if that's the case."

She actually laughs at him. "I'm not going anywhere," she tells him afterward. "Come on. We need to find a way out."

"Thank you, Stella. Thank you for not waking up and thinking I was here to kill you like you did last time at whatever hotel I'd found you in."

"You remember?" she whispers.

"Not all of it, but I do remember that part."

He helps her climb off of the bed and together they feel their way along the walls again. To think that people actually pay those popular escape rooms for this experience is more than ridiculous.

To their surprise, when they find the door, it opens with ease. It wasn't locked, latched, or even guarded when he'd nearly broken his foot trying to break through the other door.

"It can't be that easy," Stella says, following him into the hallway. Yes, it's just as dark but there is a tiny shred of lighting coming through the windows at each end.

"Should we check all the doors to find the others?" she asks.

They checked every door that they came across along the way. They were all locked, of course. The only one not locked was the one to the stairwell.

"The sign says 3rd floor," Stella tells him while holding his hand. "We were on the fifth floor when the gas hit us."

"We were on the fourth," he informs her. "Let's continue down then."

Chapter
THIRTEEN

With one hand holding tightly onto Derrick's, she follows him slowly through the second floor. "This floor doesn't haven't any rooms," she tells him. "There's two grand ballrooms and a couple of conference rooms."

"At least there is some lighting down here," he mumbles.

Derrick pulls her closer to him and she keeps up her pace. It felt right to be touching him again. There are no doubts, no animosity, no guilt, and no hurt when his skin is warming hers. Everything inside of her felt whole again.

They check the conference rooms first. All of them were empty. The frosted glass door to the major ballroom was locked as well and so was the door to the staircase right next to it. They cross the hallway to what she knows is the smaller ballroom. Even through the frosted glass door, she can see more lights shining through. Small lights like fireflies frozen in place.

"Stella," Derrick calls to her.

She looks him over and sees him in some light for the first time. "Why are you in a tux?" she asks, confused.

"Why are you wearing...*that*?!" he asks, looking her up and down.

She drops her face and looks at herself...in a dress. A white cocktail dress of lace. "What the hell?" she gasps.

Derrick swings the glass door open for better lighting and sure enough...she was in a wedding dress. A very nice and short wedding dress that she might have actually picked out for herself...if she'd planned on getting married...again.

"Is this the Russians again?" she gasps, staring at the dress.

"Over my dead body!" Derrick growls.

She'd barely connected two and two when bodies and hands shove her and Derrick into the ballroom. She screams in surprise, desperately trying to hold on to Derrick's hand. Desperate not to be separated from him because it seems fate has marked it down on its calendar that today was going to be the day.

Lights come on and things are a sea of movement. A man lands on his ass right in front of her and she gasps, ready to stomp on the asshole but a set of hands pull her back. Derrick had knocked James onto the ground and he looked completely stunned. Brooks and Jason are now trying to hold her husband's flying fists as they drag him away from her.

"CALM DOWN!" Brooks hollers out.

Derrick immediately stops his fists but keeps moving with the help of Brooks and James. Confusion takes over his handsome face. The same confusion is probably matted onto her face too.

With the lights on and the chaos died down, she scans the crowd in the room with her mouth gaped open until her tongue went dry.

Everyone that matters is here. Here in the small ballroom, dressed in their best attire. When she said everyone, she means...everyone. From all the Kings currently huddled around Derrick at what looks like an altar, most likely explaining to him what's happening, to her friends, Ben and Cael who should be in Ireland by now. Peter and his siblings are upfront and seated behind Nico and Nonna who is holding Rian in her lap.

She watches James, Jason, and Brooks sliding into the seats in the row behind the baby. They, too, are dressed their best and currently greeting Tommy and Sully. She even sees her grandfather's men, Leo and Lou, sitting and merrily chatting.

"Surprise," a gentle and warm voice says from next to her. Her grandfather, Dominic Mazzilli, takes her hand and tucks it through the crook of his arm when she faces him.

"Pop," she says. "What's going on?" This can't be another arranged marriage. Death and fire to all if he thinks that's going to happen.

"I'm here to right my wrongs. I'm here for you. It's time, Stellina. It's time you get the happily ever after a *Principessa* as you deserve. With family as witnesses," he says.

His eyes are watery and she can see his nose flushing a shade of pink. He clears his throat before he speaks again.

"I'm sorry for what I did. I know now that you are truly safe as can be and that you are loved. That's all I wanted for you just like I wanted for your mother. I'm here to show you my respect for your decision. You've chosen wisely. I cannot complain, *mio bambino*. Look at this *famiglia* you have helped build."

She had no words to say to that. No way to tell him that his being here as a guarantee that he will respect her decision has broken down so many walls.

"We'll always be family," he says, thumbing away the single tear that spills. "*Il mio sangue è tuo.*" My blood is yours.

"I'm glad you're here this time around," she tells him with a smile.

She perks on her tiptoes and gives his cool cheek a kiss, letting him hold her in his arms for as long as he needed afterward. "*Ti voglio bene, nonno. Il mio sangue è anche tuo.*" I love you, grandpa. My blood is also yours.

"Stella."

She turns around and finds a magnificently dressed Ariana standing behind her. "You knew about this?" she asks her sister-in-law.

Ariana nods her head with the sneakiest of grins. "Everyone played their part just like you've played a part in everyone's lives here. I wouldn't be where I am without you. It's the least I can do."

The tears nearly spill again with those kind words.

"No. No," Ari says to stop her. "Your makeup is still flawless right now. Let's not ruin that!" Ari looks her up and down now. "Your ensemble is missing something though."

Ariana removes her hands from behind her back to show each hand holding...magic.

"ARE THOSE FROM THE GIUSEPPE ZANOTTI WEDDING COLLECTION?" she squeals, taking the pumps from Ariana. "Oh my god! Oh my god!" She kicks off whatever the hell she was wearing before, slipping her feet into a pair of heaven's clouds, and gaining a good four inches. "Is my hair okay?" she stops and asks.

"Of course," Ari says with a laugh followed by a smile while she does a quick twirl with Dom's help. "That's more like you!"

"Are you ready to *really* do this now?" Jazzy asks from behind Ariana.

She smiles at Jazzy who looked impeccable in the most beautiful flower girl dress she's ever seen. More beautiful than the first flower girl dress Jazzy wore.

"Ariana helped me pick it out," Jazzy informs her before handing her a bouquet of lilies. "I think it's time to start because I want cake!"

And so it begins...

With soft music playing in the background, each step toward Derrick brings forth a memory of their life together. And what a life it has been. Since the beginning, since the second she sat down next to him inside the posh booth at The Whiskey Gypsy. With each step towards him, she's grows more certain that she's heading to where she's meant to be. She's meant to be right by his side.

Cael was right. Life is a series of choices, a series of forks in the road. Not every turn is going to be the right one and sometimes, there are opportunities to make a U-turn after a wrong decision. It's the destination that matters.

Her destination doesn't end with Derrick. No. Her journey continues on...with Derrick. With Rian.

And hopefully with every single person that is here to witness this ceremony. She'd left California alone. Walking down this aisle toward the love of her life, with her grandfather by her side and the small army of friends, something tells her that she'll never be alone again.

"Don't start that," Dom whispers from next to her. "You start crying. I'll start crying and then your Nonna will start in on it too," he chuckles with an encouraging and tender pat to the top of her hand.

Chapter
FOURTEEN

"I didn't mean to push you away. I just didn't know how to get us back to where we were," she whispers to her husband while dancing slowly in his arms.

Derrick places a soft kiss on her forehead. "I understand what guilt can do, Stellina. I know I tried to push you away many times before and after the explosion because of it. I know our life together is like a fucking roller coaster but I swear to you, I'd never known love until I met you."

"And Rian," she adds.

"And Rian," he repeats.

She finds Rian in the arms of his great-grandfather, sound asleep with his thumb in his mouth while Dom has rid himself of his tie, unbuttoned his top button, and is merrily chatting with Ben and

Cael. Nico and Nonna are laughing in the group next to them with Rory and Chase as well.

Adam and Ariana seem lost in their own world, dancing in a corner of their own too. Carter and Emilia are but steps away, caught in their own bubble as well. Those two really need to set a date. Something tells her that the older Ivanov brothers had a thing or two to do with that.

"Adam holds no grudges," Derrick tells her. "I shouldn't have said what I said."

She lifts her chin and faces him. "I know," she replies. "Can you believe that I actually thought you were extremely hot playing the jealous husband? I just didn't think...well, I didn't think that it would be so royally misunderstood."

"I was an idiot. I should have known that you'd have better judgment. I thought I'd lost you."

"You'll always find me. You promised."

"Always," he repeats his promise.

Someone clears their throat from next to them. They stop dancing and turn to find Peter Ivanov standing beside them with a smirk on his face.

Peter wags a brow at her before rolling his eyes at Derrick. There's a silent understanding between her and Peter. There's a connection there that she will never deny. It's a friendship more solid than gold. It's worth the weight as well. Peter knows this too so she'll NEVER understand why he likes to push her husband's buttons about it as much as he does.

"I should have let you grovel," Peter grumbles to Derrick. "Watch a little bit and see how you do before stepping in."

"You put this together?" she asks Peter.

"*Dah, ptichka.*"

"You stabbed yourself to help us?" Derrick asks in disbelief.

Peter huffs. "Don't think I'm that generous, King. The attack was real. The blood I shed was mine. But I made a good thing out of a bad after. *Thaz* all. Besides, it was your twin's idea to run with it, and then he and his wife roped in Gaston."

"Then what happened to the person who did this to—"

"It will be handled, Stella. Nothing for you to worry about. Which is why I'm standing here watching the two of you like a *suka*. Time for me to go take care of business now. My men will be here to pick me up soon. Emi and Aleks want to remain here in the States with Carter," Peter informs them.

"Thank you, Peter. They'll be safe," she swears.

She steps into his arms when he opens them for a hug. It's probably not the best thing to be doing in front of her newly re-wed husband but it's the right thing to do. No matter how rude, how crude, and how ruthless Peter Ivanov has been, he has saved her time and time again. There's a heart of gold underneath the Bratva armor he wears so proudly.

"Ivanov," Derrick grumbles.

Peter continues to hold on to her even when she takes a step back. He tilts his head and arches a brow while side-eyeing Derrick as he places a soft, lingering kiss onto her right cheek.

"I was going to thank you," Derrick mumbles under his breath.

That sentiment stole Peter's attention because her bratva friend immediately releases his arms from around her and stands up straighter with a childish grin a mile wide.

"What was that, King? I didn't quite hear so clear. Maybe your English is too fast."

"I said thank you," Derrick says cordially. He too stands up straighter, seemingly squaring up to Peter. But in a surprise move, he sticks his hand out for a shake. "You've saved my wife more than once and made sure my son was born. Thank you."

A moment passes as the two men seem to have their usual silent conversation and some sort of unspoken agreement.

"Don't let her go again. You won't have a choice next time," Peter says to Derrick. His jaw slightly ticks and he spins on his heel, confidently walking with his slight limp toward his siblings.

"What was that all about?" she asks her husband.

He shrugs nonchalantly. "I think Peter has finally accepted that it'll never be him."

"It'll always be you," she tells Derrick, her hand smoothing over the stubble on his cheek as she steps back into his arms. She rests her cheek next to his chest, next to his beating heart. "Always."

"*Sarai sempre tu,*" he counters. It'll always be you.

Chapter
FIFTEEN

Home. That's where he'd returned tonight. Not just the estate. Not just the mansion. He'd come home tonight. With his wife and his son. For the first time in too long, he didn't have to walk into an empty bedroom. He didn't slide into an empty bed and room as dark and silent as his soul used to be.

Tonight, he'd gotten in bed...with his wife.

"Your skin was perfect and flawless before me," he says, fingers tracing over a silver lining of the scar just above her waist. He kisses that scar before moving his lips onto a second. "I bled these onto you," he tells her. "You owned more of my soul each time you got one of these."

His tongue glides up her naked flesh to her shoulder, moistening yet another silver scar.

"Small price to pay to have you," she murmurs. Her eyes are glassy and hooded. She nips her bottom lip when his finger slides over her wetness, teasing her at her opening.

"You own me, Stellina. You never had to pay in blood," he whispers against her lips.

She draws his lips down to hers and just the taste of her mouth can make him release.

"I missed you, wife," he whispers against those perfect fucking lips.

"Show me," she pleads.

Tasting every inch of her body in a direct trail down to the slice of heaven in between her legs, he nestles his head with her hips squirming in his hands. Impatient little minx. He nudges her slick opening with the tip of his nose, inhaling in the magnificent scent of her arousal. He salivates imagining just what she may taste like tonight.

"Please," she pleads.

And he devours. Feasts like a caveman starved for years. Ravaging her roughly and savoring her slowly in between until he refuses to let her deny him any longer. Her pussy convulses around his tongue, her juices trailing down his chin like drool while he laps like there's no tomorrow.

When her breathing slows and her moans become whispers, he climbs on top of her, kissing the crook of her neck where a bead of sweat was resting.

"We can't do this anymore," he growls in her ear before taking the lobe between his teeth.

"What?" she gasps, her eyes widen in confusion.

"We can't keep living apart every time there's a problem, Stella. I won't tolerate it. This is the last time," he tells his little star. He won't survive this again.

"I don't want to be without you," she whispers against his lips.

He slides his body up alongside hers. In perfect unison, she slides down and turns along with him until her lips are perfectly wrapped around the head of his cock when he's flat on his back. She coats the underside of his engorged cock with her tongue, sliding him in further as her hands grab him at the base and turn the perfect twist.

A hiss escapes his clenched teeth when she takes him to the back of her throat. His perfect little dirty wife. He pumps his hips into her faster, greedily. She has one hand sprawled over his abs, scraping and scratching his muscles with her nails. Her other hand twists and moves in sync with the bobbing of her beautiful little head.

"Wife," he grunts in between breathing. "Fuck me now or I'll come down your pretty throat and keep you awake the rest of tonight, pounding into that pussy I love so much."

She stops moving on him. Her lashes bat alluringly as she taunts him with her eyes, his dick still half in her mouth. She pulls it out of her warm mouth enticingly slow then torments him even more by dragging her tongue from the base of his cock to the tip one last time.

"These games you play," he growls, pulling her up along his body.

She settles her slick pussy over his cock, giving him that mischievous smile of hers. When she slides down on him, his eyes roll up into the back of his head as if he's gotten a shot of his drug of choice, forcing him to succumb to his addiction.

"Games?" she asks as her hips move and she grinds down harder on him.

He forgets how to breathe when she starts rocking and riding him. She tosses her head back, her long hair bouncing around her each time she comes down on him. His hand traces the lines of her body up until they cup each of her breasts. They fill his hands perfectly. Soft and lush as they bounce in his hand.

He pinches each of her hardened nipples and she grinds her clit onto him, undulating relentlessly chasing her orgasm just as he's racing her for his release.

"Baby, fuck. That's it, baby."

She folds over onto his chest, her teeth sinking onto the flesh of his pec. It sets him off like a fucking geyser. His hands grip the side of her hips, pounding into her. Pushing her off of the cliff with him as colors explode before his eyes.

"Oh, FUCK!" he grunts out, trying to hold onto the moment and trying to let go of that same moment so that his body can stop trembling. It's every fucking sensation, every goddamn emotion caught in a cyclone taking him on the high of all highs.

When he returns to earth and his body again, Stella is breathing steadily upon his chest. Her arms are tucked neatly under her, in between their bodies. He places a soft kiss on the crown of her head.

Careful not to wake her, he pivots their bodies so that she slides off of him and nestles securely at his side.

Before he falls asleep, he remembers to pull the sheets over her body.

She's home. By his side again.

Chapter
SIXTEEN

"You were absolutely right, Stella. The matching outfits are the best part of the Kings' Christmas tradition!" Ariana squeals.

"I told you so. Jazzy and I always plan months ahead. We didn't have much time to do that this time around though but I think we still pulled it off," she says while she checks out everyone's grinch pajama sets.

"Do they make such a big fuss about it every year though?" Ariana asks with a frown.

She tsks at her friend and smiles. "Yep! Every. Year. But they secretly like it," she says with a wink. "Look around the room," she gestures to everyone, including Carter and Emilia since they are a part of the family too. "You don't see anyone complaining, do you?" she teases.

Ariana looks around the room now as if really paying attention to everyone for the first time. "No," Ariana replies curiously. "They don't seem to mind at all."

"See," she retorts. "I think they like to make a fuss because the Kings are nearly outnumbered now. They're getting nervous."

Ariana bursts into laughter, drawing attention from the room. Adam dashes over to his wife and then literally sweeps Ariana off of her feet.

"I don't like it when someone else makes you laugh so unabashedly, wife," Adam says with a pout at Ariana.

"Oh, puh-lease!" she teases Adam. She looks at Ariana now with a quirked brow. "See. They know their days are numbered."

"Don't hang around Stella too much, Ari. I love you the way you are and Stella tends to plant all types of seeds in people's heads," Adam jests back.

"Hey! Isn't that why you love me?" she retorts.

"Wouldn't have you any other way," he says with a grin.

Adam puts Ariana down onto her feet and steps to her, picking her up and twirling her around as if they were in a middle school playground.

"It's good to have you back home," Adam says. "The place seems too quiet without you."

"Are you saying I bring the drama?" she teases.

"The best kind," he retorts.

"Thank you, Adam. And you too, Ari," she gratefully says to the new husband and wife duo. "I really didn't know how to fix everything."

"It's our job, Stella. You're not alone in this. This is family. Your family," Adam tells her. "And because of you, our family grew by one more."

Ariana's eyes are brimming with tears now.

"No, stop that!" she scolds her friend.

"They're good tears. Happy tears," Ariana says with a smile. "I'm glad I made the cut and I'm glad that I can finally do something to pull my weight around here even though it wasn't really much at all."

"It means everything to me," she tells Ariana.

Derrick joins their group with Rian in a complete mess of cookies and cupcakes in his arms. "I think we need to get him cleaned up," her husband chuckles. "And you need to get ready to get to the restaurant."

The restaurant is hosting a special dinner tonight before their official grand opening. They will be hosting the children from the orphanage to try out their menu and for a special Santa visit. Ariana was delighted to help her put together a Kings' toy drive just for this special occasion and everyone was looking forward to it, especially the children.

She follows her husband to the grand staircase where he puts Rian on his feet. The baby has been practicing climbing the stairs lately and Derrick insists that he gets as much practice as possible. The more practice, the less he'll fall.

Watching Rian in his green grinch pajama set climb the stairs one by one probably tops the list of best Christmas memories too. At just past the halfway point, she and Derrick had to sit and take a breather with Rian who politely asked Mama and Dada to wait. The three of them sat together on those steps and people watched for far too long.

They laughed as Pam chased Brooks down the hallway with a Nerf gun. They laughed even harder when Chase skipped down the same hallway like a kid thinking that no one was watching him. The three of them snickered behind their hands when Willa had looked right and then left as she removed the elf from next to a poinsettia, the same place he sat for two days because she'd forgotten to move him.

"There goes Elfie's magic," Derrick whispered to their son.

"No touching Elfie," Rian had whispered back sternly, waggling a pudgy finger from left to right at his father. It was truly the cutest moment ever! No debate necessary.

Derrick gathers his son into his arms and she stands with them. They walk hand in hand with their son pointing out this and that through the hallway to their wing as he tries to pronounce what he was seeing. It's a picture-perfect moment.

Their life is anything but perfect. It's rough. It's grief. It's downright disappointing sometimes. But all of life's imperfections and missteps are worth it for these moments. With her love, her heart, and being surrounded by the joys of their family echoing within the walls of their kingdom.

Stronger...together.

ACKNOWLEDGMENT

My Lovelies,

    As always, thank you from the bottom of my heart for loving the Kings as much as I have loved them so far. I know many of you are needing to hear the tales of how the other Kings fall and who they will have standing by their side at the end. But this is an ever-evolving family with an incredible group of people who they call friends. Their lives are so intertwined and intermingled that everyone plays an important role in the whole picture.

    Derrick and Stella will always shine because their love and their journey became the big bang. It opened up possibilities and gave hope, leveling up the family and the empire. And just as in real life, charting new territories will come with mistakes, new friends, revisits with foes, and will bring everyone in their lives face to face with unexpected fates.

    I hope you all will continue to follow along and grow as they grow. Rise as they rise. Fall when they fall. Most of all...love when they love.

    Long live the Kings!

Always,

ABOUT THE AUTHOR

Ami Van is a crazy cat lady residing in Las Vegas, NV. As a child, she held her cats hostage in a room as she unleashed her imagination, boring them with countless stories of fire-breathing dragons and heart-shaped dandelions floating into space. Stubborn and defiant, she disregarded her tutors', teachers', and mentors' advice to explore creative writing and instead graduated college with an Information Technology degree. It took many twists and turns for her to start writing. Since she's a firm believer that it sometimes takes a little more time to find one's path, it took her nearly 16 years to finally take the first step.

For ways to keep up to date with my projects, please visit my website at **www.AuthorAmiVan.com**.

OTHER BOOKS BY AMI VAN

All links are for Amazon's US Market.

The King Family Series

Becoming His

Finding Her

Until Her

The Coin

Losing Her

Knights of Havoc MC

Dakota

Maddox

The Home Trilogy

Finding Home

Breaking Home

Coming Home

Printed in Great Britain
by Amazon